Poppleton AT CHRISTMAS

Read more Poppleton books!

Poppleton AT CHRISTMAS

Written by Newbery Medalist
CYNTHIA RYLANT

Illustrated by
MARK TEAGUE

ACORN™
SCHOLASTIC INC.

Library of Congress Cataloging-in-Publication Data

Names: Rylant, Cynthia, author. | Teague, Mark, illustrator. | Rylant, Cynthia. Poppleton ; 5.
Title: Poppleton at Christmas / written by Newbery Medalist Cynthia Rylant ; illustrated by Mark Teague.
Description: New York : Acorn/Scholastic Inc., 2022. | Series: Poppleton ; 5 | Summary: Poppleton buys presents for his friends, decorates his house with snow in a can, and shares a wonderful Christmas Eve with his friends.
Identifiers: LCCN 2018055593 | ISBN 9781338566772 (pb) | ISBN 9781338566789 (hc) | ISBN 9781338566840 (ebk)
Subjects: LCSH: Poppleton (Fictitious character) — Juvenile fiction. | Swine — Juvenile fiction. | Animals — Juvenile fiction. | Friendship — Juvenile fiction. | Christmas stories. | CYAC: Pigs — Fiction. | Christmas — Fiction. | Animals — Fiction. | Friendship — Fiction.
Classification: LCC PZ7.R982 Pwo 2020 | DDC 813.54 [E] — dc23
LC record available at https://lccn.loc.gov/2018055593

10 9 8 7 6 5 4 3 2 1 22 23 24 25 26

Printed in China 62
First printing, September 2022
Edited by Megan Peace
Book design by Maria Mercado

CONTENTS

LIBRARY

MERRY CHRISTMAS!
BAKERY

MEET THE CHARACTERS

Poppleton

Hudson

Cherry Sue

Fillmore

THE JAR

It was Christmas season
and Poppleton wanted to buy presents.

He had been saving coins in a jar
just for Christmas.

He took the jar to the store.

MENT STOR
SALE

"Now, what shall I buy for Hudson?"
said Poppleton.

He looked at things a mouse might like.

He looked at
cheese trays.

He looked at
cheese balls.

He looked at
cheese crackers.

He chose a cheese ball.

"How much?" Poppleton asked the salesclerk.

"Two dollars," said the salesclerk.

Poppleton counted out two dollars in coins.

"Hudson will love this!" said Poppleton.

"Now, what shall I buy for Fillmore?" said Poppleton.

He looked at things a goat might like.

He looked at tin cans
of peanuts.

He looked at tin cans
of pretzels.

He looked at tin cans
of popcorn.

He chose a tin can of popcorn.

"How much?" Poppleton asked the salesclerk.

"Two dollars and ten cents,"
said the salesclerk.

Poppleton counted out two dollars
and ten cents in coins.

"Fillmore will love this!" said Poppleton.

"Now, what shall I buy for Cherry Sue?" said Poppleton.

He looked at things a llama might like.

He looked at
hair spray.

He looked at
brushes.

He looked at
combs.

He chose a comb.

"How much?" Poppleton asked the salesclerk.

"Three dollars," said the salesclerk.

Poppleton counted out his coins.

He had only one dollar left!
Only one dollar for Cherry Sue's present!

Poppleton felt terrible.
He felt so terrible that he started to cry.

"Oh dear," said the salesclerk.

She called the manager.

"What's wrong?" asked the manager.

Poppleton told him about the comb
and Cherry Sue
and the one dollar in coins.

"Hmmm," said the manager.
"I say, that is a fine jar you have there."

Poppleton dabbed his eyes.
"It is?" he asked.

"Yes," said the manager.
"And we need good jars here."

"You do?" asked Poppleton.

"Would you care to sell it?" asked the manager.

"Sell it?" asked Poppleton.

"I'll give you two dollars for that jar," said the manager.

"Then I will have three dollars!" said Poppleton. "And I can buy a comb for Cherry Sue!"

Poppleton hugged
the salesclerk.

Poppleton hugged
the manager.

Poppleton hugged
Santa, who happened
to be walking by.

"Merry Christmas!" Poppleton said to everyone.

He bought the comb for Cherry Sue
and went home a happy pig.

SNOW

Poppleton wanted snow for Christmas.
But snow had not fallen.
He missed the snow.

One day he saw a can of snow in a store.

"Just what I need!" said Poppleton.

He bought a can and took it home.

Poppleton thought.

"Where shall I put snow?" said Poppleton.
"On my front porch!"

Poppleton sprayed snow on his front porch.

"Wonderful!" said Poppleton.

But soon, the can was empty.
He needed more snow.

Poppleton went back to the store
and bought two more cans.

Poppleton thought.

"Now where shall I put snow?"
said Poppleton.
"On my pine tree!"

Poppleton sprayed snow on his pine tree.

"Wonderful!" said Poppleton.

Snow

But soon the two cans were empty.
He needed more snow.

Poppleton went back to the store
and bought **fifteen cases** of snow.

"Now where shall I put snow?"
said Poppleton.

He sprayed his house.

He sprayed his yard.

He sprayed Cherry Sue's house.

He sprayed Cherry Sue's yard.

He sprayed the street.

And he sprayed Gus,
the mail carrier.

"Now it looks like Christmas!" said Poppleton.

He made a snow angel and went to bed.

MIDNIGHT

Poppleton loved Christmas Eve.
Poppleton's friends always came over
at midnight.

Poppleton called Cherry Sue.

"Are you coming over at midnight?" he asked.

"Oh yes!" she said.

Poppleton called Fillmore.

"Are you coming over at midnight?" he asked.

"You bet!" said Fillmore.

Poppleton called Hudson.

"Are you coming over at midnight?" he asked.

"With bells on!" said Hudson.

Poppleton was excited.

He put candles
along his sidewalk.

He turned on his tree lights.

He warmed some cider.

He baked some cookies.

At midnight, his friends arrived.

They gathered around Poppleton's table.

They drank cider and ate cookies.

They watched the lights on the tree.

Then they each made a Christmas wish.
The Christmas wish was always secret
and always for someone else.

After their wishing,
they took a walk.

Hudson's bells jingled.

They wished a good Christmas
to the animals of the night:
the owls,
the deer,
and the raccoons.

Then they all went home to bed
with warm memories
of a wonderful Christmas Eve.

ABOUT THE CREATORS

CYNTHIA RYLANT

has written more than one hundred books, including *Dog Heaven, Cat Heaven,* and the Newbery Medal–winning novel *Missing May*. She lives with her pets in Oregon.

MARK TEAGUE

lives in New York State with his family, which includes a dog and two cats, but no pigs, llamas, or goats, and only an occasional mouse. Mark is the author of many books and the illustrator of many more, including the How Do Dinosaurs series.

YOU CAN DRAW

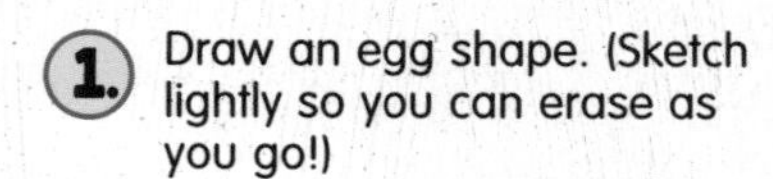

1. Draw an egg shape. (Sketch lightly so you can erase as you go!)

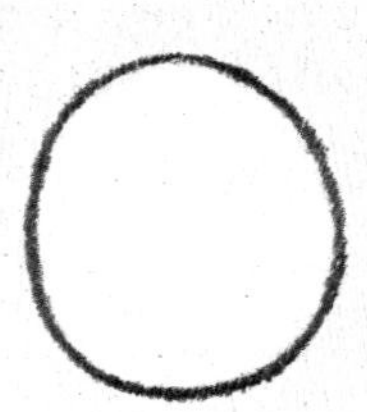

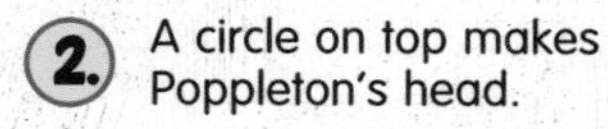

2. A circle on top makes Poppleton's head.

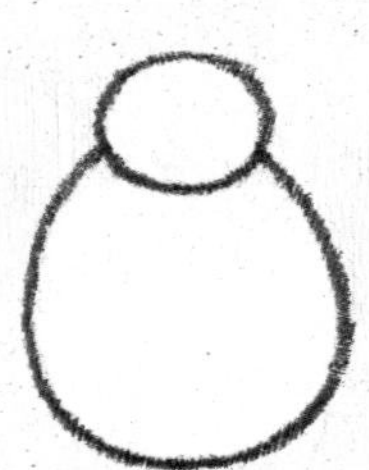

3. Add arms and legs, ears, and a snout.

4. Draw Poppleton's eyes, nostrils, and give him a big smile!

POPPLETON!

5. Sketch the outlines of his sweater. Add hooves.

6. Put a Santa hat on his head!

7. Add festive details to his sweater. That's Poppleton!

8. Color in your drawing!

WHAT'S YOUR STORY?

Poppleton saved up his coins to buy presents.
Imagine **you** have a jar full of coins.
What presents would you buy?
Who would you buy them for?
Write and draw your story!